Angelina and AJ

Visit our website at:

www.autumnchildrensbooks.co.uk

Angelina saw a mouseling dancing on Camembert's outdoor stage. She had never seen him before, so it could only mean one thing...

"That must be AJ!" Angelina announced excitedly. As they got closer, Angelina saw that AJ wasn't performing ballet steps – he was swinging his arms to a hip-hop beat.

Angelina's friend, Viki, raced over to Angelina and Gracie. "I've always wanted to learn hip-hop!" she cried out.

AJ stopped dancing. "Come on up and I'll teach you," he called. Angelina and her friends giggled excitedly.

"You need lots of energy for hip-hop," AJ told Viki.
He moved his arms up and down super fast. "This
is called popping and locking." Next he hopped
high in the air, landing on one arm. "And this is
called breaking."

Angelina couldn't wait to meet the new hip-hop kid. As soon as AJ finished his lesson and stepped off the stage, Angelina held out her hand.

"Hi, AJ," Angelina said. "I'm Angelina." Instead of shaking Angelina's hand, AJ high-fived it! Angelina giggled.

After break, Angelina and Gracie hurried to Ms. Mimi's ballet studio. When they arrived, a big surprise was waiting for them. Standing at the door was AJ!

"Come on in, AJ," Gracie said. "We love visitors!" But AJ was not there to visit, he was joining Ms. Mimi's ballet class!

AJ began performing his moves for his new classmates. Angelina was happy to see AJ, but there was one thing she wanted to know. AJ was very good at hip-hop dancing, but could he pirouette? Or *jeté* or *brisé*?

After one last stretch, Ms. Mimi had a surprise announcement. The class would perform in a *pas de deux* recital next week. "I'll tell you your partners in the next class," Ms. Mimi told them.

Angelina gulped. What if her partner turned out to be AJ?

Angelina worried about who her partner would be all the way home. When she opened the door of the Mouseling house, she was greeted by the sound of music. Angelina's little sister, Polly, was playing the xylophone and Mrs. Mouseling was keeping time on the bongos. It was just the thing to keep Angelina from worrying about the recital!

Angelina told her mum all about AJ and the upcoming recital. "I need a ballet partner," Angelina said. "AJ is a hip-hop dancer."

Mrs. Mouseling smiled. "Do you think maybe there isn't just one kind of ballet dancer?" she asked gently.

The next day couldn't come fast enough for
Angelina. She was so excited to find out who
her partner would be.

"James goes with Gracie," Ms. Mimi read from
her list. "And ..." Angelina held her breath.
"AJ goes with Angelina," Ms. Mimi finished.
Angelina froze.

Angelina knew there was only one way to find out. "Should we try the *pas de chat* first?" she asked. Angelina opened her arms gracefully over her head while AJ snapped his fingers and bounced to his own hip-hop beat.

"It might be better if you didn't snap your fingers," Angelina said nicely. She demonstrated the *pas de chat*.

AJ gave the *pas de chat* a try. This time his moves were much more ballet-like. "That's it! Perfect!" Angelina declared, feeling a lot happier.

AJ was learning super fast. His dancing was a bit different from the other ballet dancers, but it was still good!

Hip-hop had made AJ great at jumping. He showed Angelina how to leap high in the air. Angelina tried – it worked!

Angelina was having one of the best rehearsals ever. When it was time for lunch, all of the students gathered outside.

"Hip-hop, anyone?" AJ called. Before long, all of the dancers were up on the stage, doing *pirouettes* and popping along with the hip-hop kid!

Angelina felt like the luckiest ballerina in
Mouseland. AJ had taught her how to jump high
in the air and Angelina had taught AJ how to
pas de chat. Together they would make their dance
the best it could be! She couldn't wait to dance in
the recital with AJ – her new dance partner
and friend!